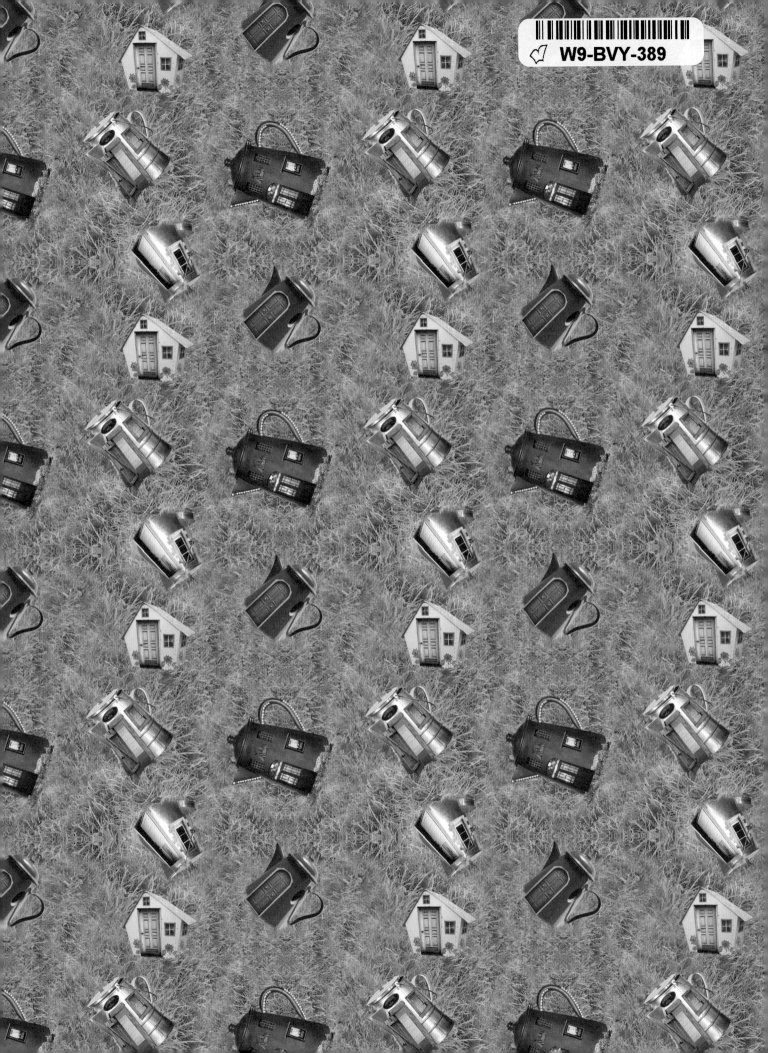

To Joshua
Love
Nonnie

I searched high and low to find that place,
I looked past hills, under rocks, and in outer space.
I found it in my imagination and thought I'd share with you,
Then you can find your SteamPotVille, too.

Look at the pictures, but try not to stall,
Then find the hidden animals, the last page has them all.
Read this strange story from beginning to end,
Then start all over, but this time pretend.

You should imagine new tales one by one,
They may be long or short, no matter, have fun.
Boys and girls are born with one exceptional skill,
To find and play in their own SteamPotVille.

But as people get older they tend to forget,
Some say their SteamPotVilles get soggy and wet.
So help the grown-ups, as a good teacher would do,
And make them tell a story right after you.

Growing up in SteamPotVille, you knew the cow said moo and the cat said meow.

The dog said roof, and the wise Indian said hau.

The bee said buzzzz,

and the bird said peep,

STEAMPOTVILLE
1000 FAERIE
BABY REDS

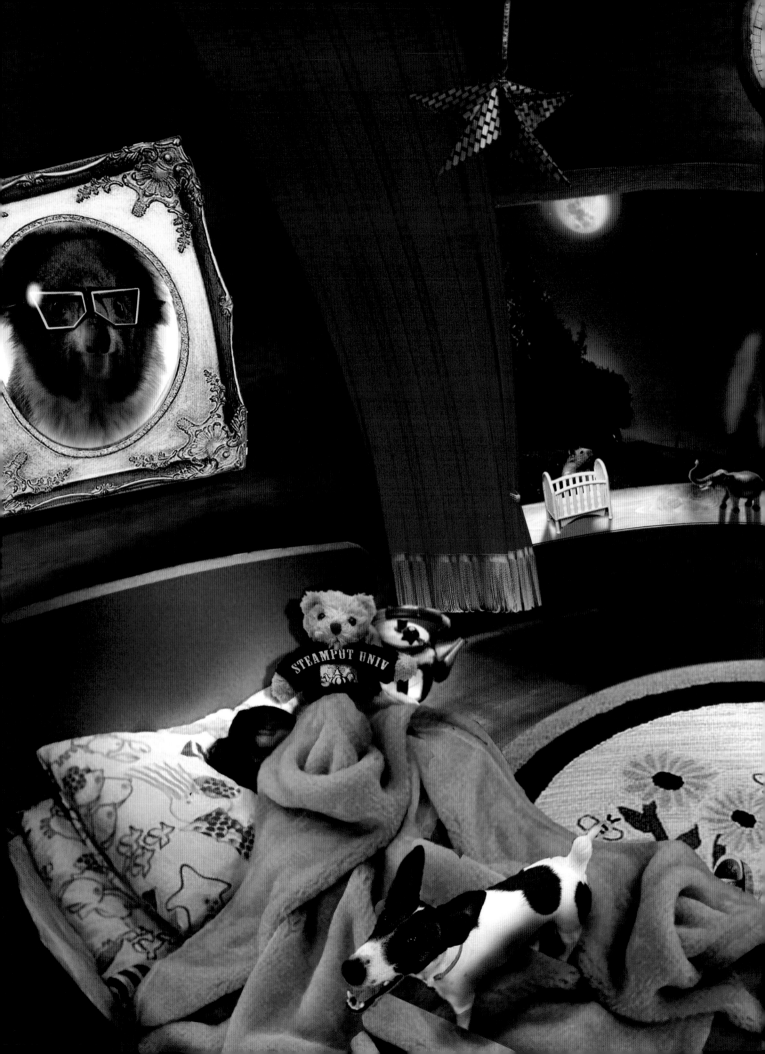

Until last night
when you fell asleep,
you had to find
the animals,
and strange things
you did meet.

The bird said buzz, wherever it was,

while the bee said peep in a hole three feet deep.

What in tarnations was going on in this town?

Why was the penguin wearing that hat?
Was froggie hiding or did he just scat?

Why were the trees spelling Hooray? And what were the Biggles doing, it's not costume day?

wo cats mooed in a room of weird stewed food,

while Uncle Chuck's jumping cow whispered meow.

Your partner the pirate parrot barked like a dog.
Well if that didn't get ya, a hippo balanced on a log.

When you found your dear friends
things weren't really right.

Someone was stealing the animals . . .
IN BROAD DAYLIGHT!

As our story goes
you didn't know what to do,
so you freed the animals
and yelled
COCK-A-DOODLE
DOO!

Then like the snap of your fingers,
things changed all around,
not-a-thing makes sense in SteamPotVille now!

But you remembered you just closed your eyes
and turned off your sight,

and when dreams come,
they come in the middle of the night.

Super-Real Hyper-Spectaculous Quite-Mezmerizing Pocket-Sized (when folded properly) Official Paper

Place hand print here.

This document verifies that _____ on such and such date, is now an official resident of SteamPotVille. This paper entitles you to hopping, jumping, and skipping anywhere you desire. Do not forget to twirl and spin on occasion.

Visit SteamPotVille any time you want to have fun. We welcome you.

Mayor Earl Gray

Name the resident and the sound it makes.
If you don't know, make it up!

VOTE
EARL GRAY

Find these animals in SteamPotVille.

Thank you to my agent Jean, and to all the people at Running Press, especially Kelli, Frances, and Chris.

Printed in China

9 8 7 6 5 4 3 2 1
Digit on the right indicates the number of this printing

Library of Congress Control Number: 2009941291
ISBN 978-0-7624-3910-2

Typography: Archer and Bureau Grotesque

Published by Running Press Kids, an imprint of
Running Press Book Publishers
2300 Chestnut Street
Philadelphia, PA 19103-4371

Visit us on the web!
www.runningpress.com
www.steampotville.com